This is a work of fiction, if

what- so- ever they ___

Warning:

May offend

☺

Tantalize

By Rayne Havok

Copyright: June 2020

By: Rayne Havok

Cover art by: Rayne Havok

One

"I know. I'll have it on your desk as soon as possible."
I leave her to ramble on, pacing by the large upstairs
window. I stop long enough to watch Steven fiddle in
his well-manicured yard. Hannah comes up behind
him, crouched over, and wraps her arms around him.

Janice, on the other end of the phone,
continues her lecture on being prompt and on time
with all deadlines. She drones one, monotone and

without vigor, as it's her main speech for the employees of the office.

I know that I have a few more minutes of this chat to make it through, so I prop my hip against the window's sill, settling in for the long hall and resigning myself to being the nosey neighbor. It's nothing I haven't done before; my bedroom window overlooks the Clark's yard.

I have tried not to make it a habit, but they have frequently become the object of my attention as of late. I've been working from home, hence my phone calls, almost hourly to Janice—the multitasking, over achieving, micro managing, boss I have on the other end, trying hard to make me her protege.

She wraps up her speech, and I give the appropriate responses that she requires to back off. I've actually already finished the task, and well before the deadline, but I can't let her know that it takes me far less time than she allots. That would be foolish.

My attention is on Hannah, looking sexy in her high wasted jean shorts, riding up on her cheeks. I hope for her to bend over so I can get a peek while I sit here a little longer than I need to, the phone in my lap now. I think again about moving my desk over to this window. It wouldn't be too difficult to switch from the one it's at now, overlooking the side yard that promises me no interruption or distraction.

I wonder again if I'd be able to accomplish anything if I were distracted daily by her pruning and watering in the garden. I saw her come out topless one time, and I've been lusting ever since. It was quick, but reminded me of being a teenage boy and hoping for the slightest hint of a nip, just one slip so I could jerk it to a real one. She walked out like some slow-moving-rock-video-girl of the 90's, flipping her hair to one side and jogging over to the end of the yard, her tiny waist and round full tits bouncy with each step. I nearly had to pull my chin off the floor. She'd grabbed the watering can and got back to the house too quickly, when she made her reappearance she was in a t-shirt.

She watered all the little pots and tended to their needs. Fully clothed, but I sat there like a creep and jacked off, picturing the way her dark nipples looked against her pale skin. The bikini-top-tan making her boobs even whiter than the rest of her. I came so hard.

Steven doesn't even know what he has in her, he's a top-buttoner, khaki pants wearing, barbeque on Sundays, limp dick nerd who I doubt could fuck her like I could. I imagine him gently lying her down and missionary-positioning her into a bored, sleepy, fake orgasm.

I'd take her hard, relentlessly pounding her insides until she screamed for me to stop, that I was too big for her. And I would be, she's so small, under 5 ft and only thick in the ways that drive me nuts.

Don't get me wrong, I'm totally infatuated with Hannah, but I've done nothing to let on that I'd take her right in front of her husband if I got the slightest hint that she was into me. As heart breaking as it is, she just is not.

Although, I have been invited to many of those Clark's Sunday BBQ's. I've gone to a handful and each one I got no indication she cared if I was there or not. Steven, ever the host, was more in tune with the crowd, making sure everyone had what they needed or wanted. She'd been nice, like always, just enough words to make you feel like you were friends, but nothing more. I'd watched her make her rounds, conversing with everyone as individuals, but they all got the same amount of time, a few words, a pretty smile, and a hand on their arm to show her affection. Then on to the next.

It's as if she did the social thing because she knew that Steven wanted it. He was in his element. And she was a good wife.

So now I'm stuck in creep-mode, where hiding behind my curtains, hoping for another glimpse of those high, round, titties is commonplace. Jacking off to the memory and hoping for a new one, all the while, trying not to let the infatuation take over completely. I'm slightly ashamed to say, it's becoming very hard to relinquish all the control my mind has, to a woman who would more than likely just laugh if she knew.

***

It only takes two full days of working exclusively from home to become full glutton-for-punishment man, and move the desk to this other window. All I kept thinking about was what was in this window while I was working at the other one. Very inefficient.

I promised myself it was to become more productive. If all I kept thinking about was whether she was in her yard or not, then moving my desk over here would answer that question instantly with a simple look. It felt like I was doing the best thing to keep my job. After convincing Janis that I could maintain my numbers from here, and that she should give the new guy my cubicle, I couldn't have her regretting that decision in the first week. So, really, I had to.

After the desk moved into the new location, and I had my first official full day here, I think it might actually be helping. If she pops into my head, I just look up. Not there. Back to work. However, there was a time she actually was there, and damn if I didn't have to watch the entire time she tended to her yard.

Wearing a simple tank top and jean shorts, doing nothing for an audience, I still couldn't look away, the easy way her tanned and toned legs moved, or the gentleness she had moving her hair out of her face drove me out-of-my-head crazy.

Steven is a lucky man.

And I am a creep.

Shaking my head and getting back to work, I realize I've spent forty full minutes watching someone water plants. I find myself so annoying sometimes. I'm a 32-year-old, not unattractive, well employed man, who, rather than even go on dating apps, would just as soon watch his very unattainable neighbor water plants. How very fucking annoying.

Despite my earlier distraction, as soon as she goes inside the house, I'm able to gather my focus and get back on task. Finally, I can feel the reprieve through my entire body.

However, the next couple of days are now spent wondering about what is going on *inside* the house.

What is she doing?

Is she bored?

Lonely?

What if I were to stop over, just for a minute—to check on her?

No.

Better yet, what if I needed something and I was just stopping by to see if she had some... sugar?

Milk?

Fuck!

So annoying.

The more I try not thinking about her, the more my thoughts hold me hostage and keep me captive there, inside and tormented. I can't even focus anymore, simply seeing her in the yard for brief moments at a time are not enough, I need to touch her, just graze her skin with the tips of my fingers, taste her neck with my mouth, smell her on me, mingling with the scent of my sheets.

I realize rather quickly; I'm addicted to her. All the responses are there, the need, the aching, and when I'm met with the unattainable, the withdrawal symptoms of irritability and anger, frustration levels through the roof.

I need my fix.

This woman will drive me crazy. If I'm not already there.

Two

I get out of the shower, and instead of heading to my desk to begin my next project, my compulsion drives me to her front door. My hair is still wet—slicked back, jeans slung low on my hips, bare feet and a thin cotton T. I'm mentally begging her to follow the porn script I've written for us in my mind.

I need her to know what to do so I can move on with my fucking life.

My hand literally shakes as I bring it up to ring her bell. Like some loser teenager picking his crush up for a date. But, fuck, I'm not even in his lucky position, I have not even gotten the "yes" to a date. I'm now more desperate than my hypothetical teenage boy.

"Gavin!" it sounds equal parts question and greeting. I try not to let it unnerve me.

"Hannah, nice to see you." I keep my eyes trained on hers and try not to give off any sexual cravings until I know what she would welcome. I've never come by unannounced, never over stepped our neighborly friendship, so I get that she's mildly put off by my being here.

Coming nowhere close to the eager slut I had hoped for, dropping to her knees to salivate all over my cock while the neighbors to watch in envy. Instead she stands expectantly, waiting for me to fill

20

her in on the reason for my very awkward and unplanned visit.

"Hey, sorry, I have been working from home." More words empty from my mouth as I try and reign in my frustration, both at her and myself. "They got a new guy and needed the space." I catch myself rambling infinitely longer than necessary, clued in by her raised eyebrows telling me that I should hurry things along.

I have never seen her act like this; at this point, if she were to be true to the character she always had been, she should have a big grin on her face and welcome me inside, maybe offer me a drink and a little hospitality. But alas, I'm on the steps and she is filling most of the rectangle entrance with her body.

Very unwelcoming.

I shouldn't have come. Damn all those pornos that have you thinking merely a drop-by would have a beautiful woman swooning with gratitude for the attention.

Hannah is definitely not a girl from Pornoville and somewhere deep in my gut I can feel the resentment curdling my insides.

What does Steven have that I don't?

Fucking nothing.

Nothing but Hannah.

Fuck him... and fuck her.

I try and stamp down my angry jealousy before it becomes apparent. I've got to follow the neighborly rules myself, even though I know it probably won't lead to sex now, but still hoping it might, I have to guard our relationship, keeping it unstrained.

"I hate to bother you, but, like I said, I'm home all day now," a charming chuckle, "I just ran out of coffee." Very original, I know, but I thought instead of handing me an ingredient she might ask me in for a cup. "If you don't mind?"

She grants me entrance with her wide, tooth-filled smile, and opens the door to me. I step inside and wait for her to lead me the rest of the way to the kitchen.

She walks ahead of me and I follow, watching her ass in a short pair of cotton shorts, her cheeks jiggling. I swallow hard and try to blink the visual into my memory and keep the lust out of my eyes so I can appear to be normal.

She reaches high in a cupboard for the coffee can, her shirt lifting and exposing the soft bare skin of her back. I nearly growl, but am able to choke it down before it becomes audible.

She spins unexpectedly. The coffee pot is in front of her and I think she'll be busy fiddling with that for another moment but just as my ass hits the stool at the bar, the coffee can is instead presented to me.

"It's all yours," she says, shoving it further toward me when my confusion stunts my ability to move.

"Oh, um, you sure?" I lift my ass slowly from the stool so it doesn't embarrass me later thinking how stupid I looked sitting down when she really wanted me to go. I take the coffee from her with graciousness instead of surprise.

"Oh, yea, Steven is so good about keeping us stocked up on things. I've got another can just waiting to be used. I notice her shuffling toward the front door; curtesy would have me follow her instead of thinking I should stay. So, I walk with her, this time by her side, as she walks us to the door.

Hannah pulls it open wide and I decide to give her one more chance to read my dirty mind. She could be very good at playing coy while inside she's begging me to give her my cock. "What are you doing today?" I blurt out, regretting it instantly after I catch the annoyance flicker across her face.

Damn, she's kind of a bitch.

She begins listing her excuses, "just have a bit of housework to get to, some laundry, and in all honestly," her voice drops to a whisper of secret, "I'm deep inside this romance novel I'm super excited to get back to." She bites her bottom lip as if embarrassed by the admission.

It goes right to my dick. So that's why she's off a bit, even rushing me out. She's anxiously waiting to get back to her porn. She's confessed to me that she's into such things, welcoming me inside that little world of hers, being so brief about it, she's encouraging me to read what I will from her reveal.

I prop my arm over my head and against the frame of the door, leaning closer toward her, with a husky and aroused voice, I say, "I couldn't very well keep you from that in good conscience." I keep my flirty, cocksure grin while she shyly thanks me.

"See you round, Hannah." Reluctantly pulling myself away as if my weight has tripled, I turn and go, purposely not looking back. I do note that the door closes a lot later than I think it should if she weren't watching me leave. I feel hopeful she may have had her eyes on my ass, which I've been told looks great in these jeans.

***

I try to get inside my house, demanding my hand remember how to operate the door knob, but the pull from her is too strong and I need to see her again already, the image of her sitting down with her dirty book is all consuming.

Leaving my newly acquired can of coffee on my porch, I turn and head for Hannah's house once again. After a bit of mental calculation, I'm sure her room—their room, would be on the side of the house opposite mine, but still in the front portion of their yard so I don't need to sneak through the gate that hides their backyard.

Good, but I'd never be able to explain my reason for being over here.

Best not to get caught then.

I keep hidden from her windows while trying to look inconspicuous to the neighborhood. Not an easy task, but important and could be vital to escape.

I feel relief when I make it to the window, in daylight, it's not smart and I have no idea how I hope to get away with this.

Brushing concern for that aside and shaking all my nerves from my body, I lean in just a tad to see what, if anything, can be seen. Just one quick look could be all I need, then I could get back home.

Please let that be true.

I've never actually been inside this room, only passed by its closed door for the restroom further down the hallway. It's nice enough, light colored walls and dark wood furniture with little knickknacks on top. Possibly a mix of both of them, female and male sharing a space. The bed is actually on this wall, there is a TV mounted opposite, I can see it's not on.

Nothing spectacular catches my eye, that is, until I see her feet, one crossed over the other. She is on the wrong side of the bed for me to see her best. But I follow them up and can see her long tan legs lead all the way to her bare thighs and it makes my dick twitch.

I can only use my imagination here, since half of her is missing, but it works perfectly to bring up the vivid pictures that make me rock hard. Taking my cock from my pants, pressing my body close to the house, becoming as small as possible, I imagine what she does when she's alone.

She turns the page, licking her finger to make the paper separate more easily. Biting her lip, she starts breathing heavy as the book gets more involved, practically writhing as the story unfolds. Hannah leans her head back on the pillow, placing the book next to her, she runs her hands across her tits and down her body. Tucking her hand into the front of her shorts, bringing her knees up, spreading them open so she can finger herself hard and fast, I hear her moaning as her gyrating hips work to fuck her thrusting fingers.

I bite down my own moan of release, keeping it trapped in my throat safe from escape. And then I splash my come on her house.

Like a pervert.

Like the fucking pervert I am.

Back inside reality, she's made no adjustments in her position while I jacked off to my thoughts. I make my escape quickly before she does, and head toward my house to mentally chastise my behavior... and probably have a cup of coffee.

Three

The days at home are getting both longer and shorter, they all seem to be running together. I either wake up in the morning groggy from dreaming about Hannah, or worse, roll out of bed exhausted after being unable to get to sleep from *thinking* about Hannah.

I get the bare minimum of work done, all while wondering about her and hoping to see her. My cock screaming in pain as I practically yank it from by body as I watch her in her garden, punishing my dick for not being able to have her. Then maybe I eat—when I think about it, and finally back to bed for the night.

This girl has fucked me up.

I need her, I need to feel the inside of her, make her wet, just have her on my body.

So, when Steven sent an invite to this Sundays barbeque, I didn't hesitate to accept.

***

I salivate at the sight of her opening the door for me, the little summer dress is white and pale pink, accentuating her tan and shifting my cock into overdrive.

"Gavin," she smiles and opens the door wide for me, I watch as her body shifts and her muscles work. I'm fucking hard over the subtlest of gestures her body makes.

I intentionally brush against her, even though there is plenty of room for me to maneuver around her. She follows me out to the yard, after which I watch everything she does, admonishing myself for being so fucking obvious.

In an effort to keep as inconspicuous as possible, I try to mingle with everyone else. I've met them all before at one or another Clark barbeques. The conversation is easy, letting them at the helm, steering the topics wherever they may want to take them, generally—and not the least bit surprising— about themselves. I'm content to let them think it's important stuff while using only half smiles and nods.

Steven comes over, Hannah on his arm. She took his—which irks me. But she's in front of me, standing close enough to smell the summer on her skin and for now that's all that matters.

"Gavin, glad you could make it, these Sundays are the highlight of my week. Always glad to see you." Steven shakes my hand with the grip of a car salesman.

I muddle my own words back, unable to pry my eyes from Hannah's mouth, her tongue is working the back of her teeth, her mouth open just enough to watch it. Sliding her tongue over her lips, top and then bottom, leaving behind glistening saliva, my eyes close briefly to saver that memory to replay over and over.

I can't help but think she is putting on a show just it for me, she can see I'm watching practically agape. She's blatant and overtly sexual, one might even be able to imagine the nasty things she's thinking to display such an act. Aside from coming out and saying she wants to fuck me with her mouth, this is nonverbally a promise of it.

Fuck yes.

Steven pays no mind, waving to someone behind him; he excuses himself and leave us alone together.

"So," I try to formulate a sentence, something interesting to fill the void, but that's all I got.

"You're so funny, Gavin," she giggles and moves her hand to my forearm. She's done this countless times, but this time she squeezes a little and my dick takes over all ownership of my mind and body, announcing his presence by shoving against my fly.

She obviously walks away after that, I would too, I'm not behaving like I normally do, or like I should be. I'm a fucking horny teen, ogling an older woman, although she is not, she's 25, practically new to life. I should be the influencer here. I should be able to be the grown up. Instead I'm tongue tied and nervous, with a raging boner that is awkward to say the least.

I stay for only enough time that it doesn't seem like I'm running from the incident, and then watch from my window as she flutters around her beautiful yard, tending to all the guests able to maintain themselves like gentlemen—not like perverts looking for a corner to slink away and jack off into.

Recognizing that I'm speaking from circumstance, and true to my perversion, I stoke myself as I imagine little beads of sweat dripping down her throat, cascading between her breasts, her hand swiping the droplets away. I swallow hard, trying to make the fantasy last so keeping my touch light, my grip loose.

But when she looks up at my window, so abruptly that there is no mistaking what she's doing, what she could be seeing, her eyes going straight to mine and hold them, even from my second story window I can see her stare and the flirty smirk telling me she knows what I'm doing and that she's more than ok with it.

My hand tugs my dick harder, wrapping tighter, and so much more audacious. I need to come with her eyes on mine, releasing the tension in streams of hot come shooting across my desk, the papers and my laptop are covered. And still her eyes remain upturned and on me.

Through the sheer curtain, I imagine she can't see too much, but I'm not stupid enough to think she can't see me when I can see her. And her small, satisfied smile confirms she had seen enough. The flip of her hair and she switch in her hips tells me she may have even liked it.

Four

Hannah is making it nearly impossible to get anything done; my brain is practically full of her. If I could just get a taste of her, I'm sure I could alleviate this issue, possibly even go on with the rest of my life with some dignity.

I've always been able to get over any woman from my past—no problem, I simply had to sleep with them. That itch finally scratched, the wonderment and lust quenched, and it's all of a sudden not the most important thing going on in my head. They were vanquished and I was no longer tormented. That's what I'll need now to get my reprieve.

The tricky part here is that Hannah is married, and although she appears to be alluding to something, there doesn't seem to be a chance in hell for me... yet.

I don't want to ruin what the Clark's have if I just need a bit of her, just her body, not her mind, or her fucking breakfast preferences. I just want to feel her insides. That's what I need. Steven can have the rest.

And so, my dilemma becomes apparent, in my effort to mollify this craving, I don't think she'd be the type to give it up to me and then go back to her daily norm. Plus, I am next door, so it would probably be too much for her conscience, eventually having to confess all to Steven, ruining my quiet, simple life.

Now, I'm no sicko, just a man with a little too much Hannah on his mind. The thought of her driving me closer to insanity. I have to do something. And I've deduced it must leave me anonymous. In every sense, I'm thinking even anonymous to Hannah herself.

Steven informed me at the barbeque a couple weeks ago that he'd be heading to Florida for a week, that he'd like for me to keep an eye on the house. I think knowing he'd be gone made this whole thing worse. It spun my mind and looped an awful thought into it. One I'm thinking is the best option for us all to get back to our lives.

I haven't finalized the entire plan yet, but I have two days to get it perfected and an entire week to take advantage of it. Or, I'm thinking, forever hold my peace. If I can't do this, then the next option, with the furious way my mind reels around her, is simply going mad and getting a nice little room with padded walls and lots of fun medication.

The question being, am I receptive and open-minded enough to be able to sneak into her house and rape her? Am I capable of becoming a rapist?

I have chosen to actually use the word in my mind, not to sugar coat it at all. Because when it's finally time to do it, I want to be able to go through with it. I don't want the shock of it all to hit me then and scare me off. I need to go in there and actually rape her, to be her rapist.

Just fuck her until my dick has had the taste and can surrender my mind. Only once, it's all I'll need, and then back to normal.

I don't think I'm a creep, I'm simply a man trying to do what's best for everyone involved. I don't want to ruin her marriage or take her from her husband—however boring he is. I don't want to have move, or rearrange my, or their, lives at all. Honestly, this is the most responsible way to go about it.

I'm not a creep.

I'm a thoughtful man.

A forward-thinking man.

This will be simple. I'm convinced of it.

The reel of visuals begin again, inspiring all the nerves in my body start moving. I'm so excited for her.

***

Thursday morning, from my bedroom window, I watch Steven load up the car in his driveway. Coming down and going to my mailbox at the end of mine when I know he's getting ready to head off.

"Gavin, hey," he jogs over to my side of our connecting yard. "Hey, I'm leaving this morning, I really appreciate you keeping eyes on the house. Good neighbors are hard to find." Another of those car salesman handshakes threatening to amputate my fingers.

I nod and smile, concentrating on keeping the whirling thoughts of Hannah being under me from showing on face, the eagerness at bay.

Steven finally relinquishes my hand and I flex my fingers in an effort to recirculate blood to them. "It was going to be a week, but its only two days now, the conference is being condensed. We all thought it was a bit much to ask everyone to be gone from their homes for a full week. So, I'll be home Sunday."

"That's great. I can hold down the cul-de-sac until then," I chuckle, but to my ears, I can only hear the anxiety in it. That amped up my schedule, which makes be both jittery and wildly excited. I feel the urge to shove him inside his car and push it down the driveway, but I hold back, waiting for him to drive away so I can wave like a good neighbor instead.

I catch sight of Hannah as I turn to go in, standing tucked inside her front door, waving her own goodbye. She's only wearing an oversized t-shirt and the loud scream of overflowing sexual frustration rings between my ears where only I can hear it.

***

I can't do anything the first night, I know that, they'd know for sure it was an inside job and someone with intel obviously did it. So, the first night, I go through the plan, mulling it over in my head until it becomes routine—and my cock a little raw from my hand.

Hannah has kept to her mundane routine; I'm watching her in her yard. This afternoon she is in a bikini top and a pair of black shorts which is not unusual, but it still makes me feel like a virgin in high school, every bare inch of skin tugging my cock.

She drags a lounge chair to the center of the yard and positions it into the flat, reclined option, so she can lay on her tummy.

A flood of hostility rushes in from nowhere and I silently beg her to just go the fuck inside her house. It's all become too much for me, the pinnacle reached, and now edging toward something else entirely. But she doesn't listen to my telepathic pleading. Instead, doing the complete opposite, she pulls the string on her top—so as not to get a tan line—and hikes her shorts into her ass crack like some witch tantalizing me.

For fuck's sake, it's as if her mission is to have me punch through the wall and pounce on her right now.

I stand, with my forehead pressed to the cool glass, and concentrate on her breathing. I imagine licking up her spine to her neck, collecting the little beads of sweat that cover her, tasting the saltiness of her sun-warmed flesh.

She reaches behind her and reties the strings, when she rolls to her back, she is completely covered, expert level repositioning—not even a nip slip. Folding the elastic of her shorts down low, she's able to keep all the best parts hidden.

Fuck her modesty.

I'm so annoyed at her right now for not taking this opportunity to bare herself in the solitude of her secluded yard. All alone for the weekend, she's still unable to let herself be free to enjoy herself.

I take my mounting anger out on my cock. I'm unable to restrain myself, she is infuriating me right now. I need her to reach into her shorts and finger-fuck herself, but she doesn't. I need her to grab her tits and squeeze them, arch her back and grind her hips, so horny she can't stand it. But she just fucking lies there, forcing me to come with only my imagination.

Again.

Five

It's nearly pitch dark outside, the moon is slivered, the stars abundant. I'm no longer worried about someone catching me creeping into the Clark's yard.

This can finally happen.

I practically died last night from impatience, knowing Hannah was all alone. The smart part of my brain knowing that I needed to hold off until right now, that it was imperative to follow the rules and the plan.

No deviations.

That is the one absolute.

So now is the time, the objective is clear, and everything is going to go as planned. All I have to do is focus on what I want the outcome to be and bring it to fruition.

I can do this.

I'm ready.

I'm dressed in dark colored clothes, making my way to the window that will let me peer into the Clark's living room. When I don't see her there, I imagine she's already in her bedroom.

Sneaking in the darkest of shadows over to that window, careful not to stumble or make any noise to sound the alarm, I inch forward.

I made it a point to unscrew the light bulb, that is motion-activated, the other day, realizing that it could have been my downfall if left forgotten or neglected.

I make it here easily enough, peering inside and around the curtain left with just a sliver of an opening. I catch sight of Hannah's reflection from the mirror in her bathroom. She's at the sink wearing a t-shirt and nothing else. This, I've come to realize, is her pajamas.

Presently, she is furthest from the front door, so when I sneak over to it now to ring the doorbell, I know I'll have enough time to make it through the window I've jimmied and into my hiding spot before she's made it back to her room again.

I thought that ringing the bell would be best, the house is too small to sneak around unheard, having the sound of Hannah's footfalls envelop my own is the perfect cover.

Plus, I kind of like the idea of her being on guard. Yes, it could be young kids fucking around at her door, but it could also be me.

Settling in, having made sure to get everything back the way it was before shimmying through the window, I get comfortable—as comfortable as one large man can be inside a small closet.

She's back in a few minutes, carrying a snack plate with some cut-up fruit on it and a glass of water.

Clicking the TV on, she settles under the covers, head propped against too many pillows left at the headboard, and watches some talk show. I figure she's tucked in for now, so I hunker down in the closet, door slightly ajar, and watch her watching the show. The smile on her face lit up by the glow of the screen, laughing when it's the more obvious jokes. She giggles and crunches her food while I wait.

The host is just about to introduce a new guest when the screen announces a countdown for the sleep timer, flashing numbers descending from thirty, finally going dark when it reaches one. Only then do I let myself get excited.

I give it a full twenty minutes more, running the plan through again, making it very clear that she is asleep. Her soft breathing—not a snore, but a heavier version of breath, deep and melodious. Possibly the most relaxing sound on earth, keeping my heartrate in normal range, and soothing my anticipation. I have her to thank for being my calm before her storm.

Soundlessly moving the door open, I keep my eyes trained on Hannah. She is faced away from me, lying on her side. I take my sweatpants off and leave them crumpled in a ball on my shoes. After silently leaving my hiding spot, I unroll the condom onto my already hardened cock to keep my DNA from becoming a part of the scene.

It feels good to think that this is finally happening, my dick hasn't been in a resting position for weeks. I can't fucking wait for this release, she is the epitome of my decline in sanity, embodying everything I need to conquer to get back to my façade of normalcy.

The next part has to be done quickly. Even though it's mostly dark in here, I can't count on that being good enough for my anonymity, thusly defeating the entire purpose of all of this.

Slipping the pillow case I brought from home, brand new and opened only after I had my gloves on, over her head. I'm able to hold her still fairly easily when she awakens startled and begins to struggle. I tighten a large zip tie around her throat to keep it in place, but with enough room for her to breathe easily enough. Then, using the smaller one around both of her wrists, I hold them above her head, dragging her legs over the edge of the bed, presenting her ass to me.

After removing her tiny panties, I try to take my time, slipping my fingers into the opening of her pussy, the slickness between her lips—I know is not for me, but it is there and she smells sweet. I want to taste her, but I can't get my saliva on her.

I do take a moment to finger her and rub her against my latex-covered cock. Feeling the heat coming from her insides, warm and welcoming. I shove in to her, burring my cock deep inside her hot hole, every inch of me sheathed.

I push into her, trying to make her enjoy this so I can hear what she sounds like when she's fucked, but there's nothing. She's silent whether I'm slow or fast and it's infuriating me.

Not even a scream, she just lays there as I try to coax anything from her. I take my hand from around her wrists and she keeps them above her head without prompting.

She's passive and meek, maybe she's too scared to react, maybe this is what they teach women to do if there is someone raping them. Who the fuck knows, all it's doing is making me mad.

Grabbing a fist full of her hair I wrench her head up toward me, changing the gruffness of my voice, I almost growl into her ear, "you better fucking hope I'm satisfied with this or I'm coming back."

She whines when her head hits the mattress but remains quiet otherwise. That, coupled with the fact that this condom is making it impossible to feel anything, I'm getting fucking pissed.

My thrusts are rougher than I wanted them to be, my aggression is overflowing. My cock needs the attention it's been demanding. I need more from her—anything really! and she's giving me fucking nothing.

Gritting my teeth, I kick her legs apart and use both my arms to pull her hips into me with each thrust, as little as she is, I know this hurts. I relentlessly pound her until finally she cries, breathlessly begging that I stop. At last, I feel something in my dick. Reaching from the depths of my soul, I come hard inside the condom, wishing I could be filling her tenderized hole.

Slipping my cock from her slowly, milking the last of my come into the receptacle, I let her feel relaxed enough to think this is over. She doesn't have to know that I have more in store for her just.

Tugging off the used condom and knotting it. I get another out of my shirt pocket and slip it on, I'm still hard enough to go again right now. I have a month of pent up torment from her. Tantalizing me with her alluring innocence and forbiddenness. Practically begging to be looked at and fucked, and then offering nothing after the hook was in.

I'm seething again at the thought of it all, so frustrated that she's done this to me.

She's turned me into a rapist.

A fucking creep.

Peeping tom.

And an angry dick torturer who's had to resort to countless hours of solo tugging, like an ugly fucking reject, who isn't worthy of her magical, stupid, fucking pussy!

Unable to lube her asshole with anything, not even my spit, I try to force my way inside with only the slickness of the condom. Her legs thrash and she struggles to scurry up the bed and away from me, but I am faster. Wrapping my arm around her waist, I lift her up and shove her body hard against the wall and enter her.

Fucking her ass hard while trying to reach a level of satisfaction that will alleviate this ache in my balls, she screams and I don't try to silence her, I relish the tears, I crave more of them.

She created me.

My cock hunts for relief. Deeper and deeper I root inside until I feel a slickness that I can only attribute to her bleeding, and that's what finally undoes me. I needed to hurt her like she's been hurting me. I come, from the deepest parts of my balls, I feel the release and it makes me moan in a way that tells me I've done it.

I got what I came here for.

Letting Hannah go, her body slides down the wall and onto the floor. I move around the room, collecting everything I need to leave with, pants and shoes back on, two condoms with wrappers accounted for.

Leaving her as is, covered with the pillow case that will not lead back to me, mewing on the floor, unable to move. I walk out the front door, ensuring I won't fumble getting out it or accidently leave anything behind, closing it tightly.

Sneaking back into my house through the side yard furthest from her house, I toss the incriminating things into my burn-bag and get inside the house unfettered.

It's cool enough that no one will think it's strange that I have a fire burning. I started it before I left, so you couldn't even say it was befitting of this reason. I toss the whole thing in, watching for a moment as the edges start to singe. Finally stepping into the shower, scrubbing hard and using more soaps than any of my ex's ever have. The bathroom is a cloud of condensation that I wipe from the mirror.

I feel as though that may have been exactly what I needed, that it should bring me back down and make it possible for me to live outside the obsessive loop of Hannah's torment.

The red and blue lights strobing through the window put a quickness in my step. A multitude of car doors slam, letting me know there is more than a couple cruisers arriving.

White lady in low crime rate subdivision, better send the best of the best. I was prepared for this.

I turn the hair dryer on so it's not so obvious I am freshly showered. Then I throw on a pair of basketball shorts and go downstairs.

Rubbing pretend sleep from my eyes as I pull the door open and put on my best impression of 'guy who was in bed, woken by the ruckus' act.

Standing on the top of my three-step entryway, I holler to the police officer closest to me who had already been made aware of my appearance when he caught me open the door. "Sir?" I thumb over to the Clark's house, confusion and concern in my voice. "What's going on over there?"

"You know your neighbors?" he asks, pulling a notebook from his chest pocket as he walks over to me. Stopping at the bottom of the steps, looking at me as though he can see through any line of bullshit I feed him, so I better make it the truth—all done with a simple lift of an eyebrow, clicking the pen a few times just to make sure it's functional.

He's good, I'll give him that and things are going about exactly as I thought they might.

"I do, Hannah and Steven Clark. Been there at least the three years I've been here. What's happened? Please." Urgency in my voice and worry on my brow.

"It seems we had a break in. You wouldn't happen to have seen anything would you? Anyone in the neighborhood looking suspicious. I'd say," looking down at his too-fancy watch, "about half an hour ago?"

"Oh man, no, I was in bed, watching TV. Is everything ok? Steven is out of town. I was supposed to keep an eye on the place." Time now, for regret and worry.

"She's going to be fine; it looks as though it might have been more a personal attack, nothing appears to be taken. So, when you say 'keep an eye on the place', what does that entail, exactly?" his lips pucker as though he's really trying to make me see his curiosity.

"Oh, you know, in the way you kind of say it, but don't really mean it. I wasn't supposed to do anything but passively keep an eye out, you know?"

"Yea, sure, so you didn't see anything strange?" as though he realizes I wasn't meant to be an armed guard, ready to disarm any foe who may find his ass on the wrong side of the Clark's door, and more plainly a neighbor just keeping it copacetic, he seems to relent.

"Nothing at all, I'd be the first to investigate it too." I try to put on a macho tough guy act, like I'm more one of the boys than an evil neighbor dirty deeding the block. I'm only here to be on the record that I was home and get my alibi together. Could there be a better way to do that than having a blue-blood vouch for me?

"Good for you," tucking his cop-props back into his pocket, "although if you see anything later tonight, just give us a call, best not to confront someone like this. It was pretty brutal."

Before he turns to go, I come out into the porch light more, showing that I've got no visible marks on my shirtless body, if they're wondering if she fought or scratched her assailant, they won't look at me suspiciously. I'll have a cop who saw me mere moments later with no signs of a fight.

I should be all clear and they can find the miscreant elsewhere.

"Thank you for doing what you do. I know you can't get there before it happens, but I appreciate you making it your mission to catch the fuckers who do this."

He tips his hat at me and nods. "It's what I was born to do."

Ok bro.

"Do you need anything else from me?" Walking down the steps as if I've been called upon to join the force just then.

He holds up a hand to stop me, gently breaking it to me that I'm not on the team, "I'll let you know."

"Do you think she'd need a visitor or something?"

"I think it's just going to be a bunch of tests, she mostly is ok, but I'll make sure she gets home with a female officer when they release her. Maybe then would be a more appropriate time for visits."

"Ok." I leave it at that, I want it to be concern and not menace that he sees. I've watched enough crime shows to know what they look for to latch onto you and paint you as 'the guy'.

For a moment I watch as he walks back to Hannah's house. I still have yet to see her. Curiosity calls to me for a brief moment. I am a bit intrigued to see if I hurt her, but not enough to seem like a looky-loo to the police, who I'm very certain still have their eyes on me, so, instead I retreat into my quiet house and squash my wonderment.

Lying with my hands tucked under my head, replaying a bit of the good parts from tonight. Focusing mostly on the scent of her. Her hair smelling of fresh strawberries and her skin subtly fragranced by something plucked from a summer-bloomed flower. I finally relax enough to go to sleep; it seems the first night in months that it happens so naturally.

Finally.

Fucking zen.

Six

I don't see Hannah for three entire days, and within that time I'm able to reorient my thoughts, putting her further down and out of my mind, after the first day of her not coming outside to tend to the yard, I didn't look as frequently the second, and then by the third, she was nearly gone. That is... until she wasn't.

The split second my eyes caught her it all came flooding back. She shoved her way forward and trapped me again inside that obsession, my thoughts smothered with her. The invasive way she holds me captive inside my own mind is the most wicked thing that's ever been done to me. How can someone wield that much power over another? It should not be a possibility, yet, here I am, subservient to her every move.

Steven's car has not left since it all happened, he had returned home early that night and not left Hannah's side since. Even having groceries delivered, which although super convenient, seems a little over the top.

What is it about her?

Let the man breathe.

He seems to be the doting husband, tending to her every whim. I caught up with him outside as we both checked the mailboxes at the curb.

"How is she doing? I can't even imagine what it must be like for you two. I'm so sorry I wasn't there." All the words tumble out. I try to sound remorseful for not ensuring her safety in his rhetorical ask to keep an eye out. All while trying to get an update on how things are, and possibly, if they'll return to some sort of normalcy soon.

"Hannah's hanging in there. Recovery from something so brutal isn't all physical, she's got a lot of healing to do, mentally too. She's really shaken up. She won't let anyone see her right now. She doesn't want the home invasion, or the reason for it, to linger in people's memory, let alone have the visual of it to facilitate that. Poor thing." He shakes his head sympathetically.

"I bet, I'm so sorry, Steven."

"I've taken a leave of absence from work; I have about a month of paid time to take advantage of, so we should be ok. She doesn't want to be left alone right now. It's so hard for her." If I'm not mistaken, I see the swell of tears collect before he's able to blink them back.

"If you, or Hannah, need anything please let me know, whatever it is. I'm right next door." I clear my throat, letting on that it has also choked me up.

I stand there watching as he shuffles off, moving for my own door only after I see his close behind him. I can't help but think of what she doesn't want people to see. I don't remember hurting anything physically—maybe her insides, but it seems, there may have been something else.

I feel a twinge of guilt, but then I remember it was she who drove me to it. If she wasn't so tantalizing, so fucking obnoxiously present in my mind, this whole thing could have been avoided.

I rush inside for a much-needed shower, not the kind that gets you clean, the kind that clears your head. Irritation builds quickly at the thought of

Steven there babysitting for an entire fucking month. If things don't return to normal soon, I fear the agony of it all will compound and fill me so full of need I'll overflow again, this time things could get worse.

Could they get worse?

Oh fuck, what if it got worse?

I punch the wet tile in the stall then rush out of the shower without grabbing a towel. Marching to the window, forcing my desk out of the way to get the closest view available, I press my dripping forehead to the glass and will her to step out into the yard.

This morning was the first I'd seen Hannah since our night together. Her head hanging down, a nest of messy hair draped across her shoulders and covering her face. Wearing a terrycloth bathrobe— something she's never done before. Nothing remarkable about it, but it was all it took to get me fixated again. Surely, it couldn't be anything other than black magic. Her spell is working better than ever and it's becoming harder for me to remain a gentleman.

Some sloppy, torn down version of the sexy neighbor girl had been enough to fuck me up again. And now, I'm practically shaking from withdrawal.

Knowing it will take a long time for her to get back into her routine to satisfy me for another short while.

But what happens after that?

What she drove me to do then will not be an option this time, not only was it not as satisfying as it could have been—to be inside of her but not really feel her, to have to wrap my dick in latex. Not be able to taste her without leaving a trace of my saliva behind. But it would also be a greater coincidence than is allowed, making it overall not worth it.

It's time I came up with something else. If Steven weren't there, I'd be able to get closer to Hannah in her time of desperation. I know she doesn't have any family to turn to, and that it would leave the door open for her friendly neighbor to swoop in and help her out in her time of need while not being the least bit judgmental.

The puddle of water at my feet tells me I've been standing here long enough. I put a mental list together of the things I've been neglecting around the house and prepare to block out all thoughts of her reeling in my mind. Nothing can be done about her yet.

After hours of exhausting chores then mowing and pruning my own yard, I'm beat.

Another shower, this time to clean up instead of alleviate the life squeezing pressure of Hannah, is needed before I climb into bed completely naked and sprawled out. I stare at the ceiling fan whirling slowly, hypnotically, my brain wanders and sleep steals me.

I wake, same position, drenched in sticky sweat and shortened breath.

The vivid recall of my dream... or could it be reality? Confusion about the validity propels me to the front door, yanking it open, I confirm Steven's car is still parked in his drive. The dream becomes more obviously a figment again. Taking my naked ass back into the house, leaning hard against the door to close it.

He's not dead.

He's not dismembered and buried in my freshly maintained yard. He's next door for the foreseeable future, protecting the woman who is driving me mad.

Much like real life, in my dream, I was at the end of my rope. I got thinking that if Steven was dead, I could either get closer with Hannah, or, and this was equally welcome, it drove her away to some undisclosed location, far from my mind. Letting me return to my life. Both were equal and acceptable conclusions. Such a relief that I know it needs to happen. I need to push her over the edge and out of her comfort zone so she does something.

I need to upheave her life and let her free of him and over to me or completely gone. Then my mind can rest.

So, although I am not a stalker, I am stalking. Although I'm not a rapist, I have raped. Now, it seems, although I'm not a murderer, I must do just that.

This girl is so fucking annoying.

Seven

The plan is hatched, the last couple of weeks I've gotten the habits of next door. Albeit, from the safety of my own plot of land. Just observation but as daunting and slow as it is, it has lessened the stress. Just knowing that I have a plan to look forward to, an ending to all this torment has been quite a relief. I'm even sleeping better, the dreams are a bit awful, but who am I to begrudge my wish for the past sleepless months?

On Wednesdays Steven is leaving for a few hours in the early morning, thusly making it my only time to strike. I don't know where or why. He returns with nothing indicating his adventures.

Hannah has not come out as often and the one time a saw her face it was bruised, swollen, and looked horrible. It also turned me on, so add that to the list of shit she's making me—a sexual deviant who is proud of his handy work. Add in a little resentful that it's her only suffering while I'm here in anguish every moment because of her for good measure.

***

The days are long, as I watch them pass for Wednesday's turn. This morning I'm waiting for Steven to join me in his car, the fact that he doesn't know I'm here is my advantage.

Sitting inside the cramped trunk, I wait. While he slept, I dismantled the backseat so it looks intact but leaves me a way to emerge behind him with no noise when I move the cut-away seat aside to slide in behind him. Making my presence known only when the time was right for the attack.

Last night I had left the house in my own car and drove to a spot I think will be perfect, its centered such that if he goes left or right at this intersection, it would still be ok, it being the only way into our development heightens my odds.

Pulling the car off the road and hiding it behind a lush line of trees to block it from the road. Leaving it there, I walked home to get the rest taken care of just in time.

It is important that I'm not seen near the crime scene or with the victim. I needed it known that I left my house before Steven disappeared—

hours before. And that I returned hours later, leaving zero question about my having time to do this.

The subtle curve of the road tells me that it's time. Slipping into position, I make my presence known with a gun to his head.

I tell him to pull over.

He jerks the wheel at the sudden sound of a voice. The car swerves but he recovers, slamming the breaks hard, skidding to a stop on the gravel berm next to the road.

Stuttering with no actual words forming, he suddenly stops and I see it piece together for him.

"Yea, I know…right?" I say.

He looks pissed, like he wants to kill me. I can't blame him. Not only did I get over on him once, and have my way with his woman, I snuck in again to take even more from him, and all without the slightest bit of speculation thrown my way.

I force him out of the car and I follow behind. "Walk," I demand.

"Why are you doing this to us, Gavin?"

"Trust me, I don't want to be doing this, but it's got to be done." I can't very well go into how I've become obsessed to the point of no return with his wife. It's not that simple, nor is it his business.

We make our way deeper into the brush, both tall enough to hide us, and thick enough to make it super fucking annoying to walk through. I stumble and nearly fall. I think of how horribly that could have ended, I fall and drop the gun, he takes it, and either kills me, or takes me to police.

Brilliant.

I decide now is the time, no more unnecessary risk. Without a word, I shoot him. Blood sprays out of his head and globs of disgusting warmth hit me in the face.

That was unexpected.

I should have worn a mask or something. But in fairness to my naiveite, I didn't know brains did that.

Next time.

Will there be a next time?

What if there is a next time!

His fall interrupts my tangent. It's over. I feel a relief that lets my mind rest.

Finally.

Step one done.

Dragging him to my car is an event, both arduous and challenging. But we make it before the tugging dislocates my shoulders. After wrapping his head in a large bag to contain most of the bloody mess that seems to be oozing more than I want it to, I load him into my trunk, which I've meticulously lined with plastic for easy and thorough clean up.

Taking my clothes off and splashing what remains of an old plastic water bottle from the backseat over my face to get this shit off of me. I shove the clothes into another burn bag and redress in clean clothes that are exactly the same as I left in—in case I was seen leaving.

Stopping the car alongside Steven's, I douse it with an accelerant and toss a book of matches to light it up. Driving slowly, I ensure it's fully engulfed before I drive quicker. Watching the plume of smoke build from the rearview mirror as I get further away.

I pull into the garage and shut the door quickly. Unloading Steven, I make sure there is no trace of him in the trunk and then set him aside.

I figured I needed to bring him back here; I wanted the car found but not the body. I wanted the wonder and confusion.

Did he run off?

Where's the body?

Did someone do this to him or did he do this?

The more directions the police have to go in, the busier they will be. I couldn't involve anyone else in this, so no friend who has connections to a guy who crushes cars, no friend to help burry the body in a remote area that promises no animals could get to Steven, no internet searches to find out what liquid I could use to dissolve a body.

The list went on.

It's safer just me. Burn the car that I can't hide. Take the body, that could have a trace of me on it, and put it where I know it won't be found. I'd hate to have to keep driving to another location to check that he's still buried. Best just to have him close.

The hole I made for Steven is deep enough to keep the stench, hopefully. Again, new territory, this is all speculation.

After dragging him toward it, wrapped in the plastic from the trunk, I shove him in. I spend the next two hours refilling the giant hole and replacing the grass sod chunk I had carefully removed, tucking it all neatly together again.

Utterly spent I fall asleep quickly, mud covered and grimy. I have nothing left in the tank.

This bitch better be worth it.

Eight

Hannah...

He'd made me suspicious for a while, but how could my neighbor having a little crush on me lead to this?

After Steven left this morning, I headed over to Gavin's house through the backyard for a little look around. Call it shock, if you will, but I narrowly missed plunging head first into a hole in the ground.

Now, I don't want to be presumptuous, but, like, a body-sized hole.

And it freaked me out, as any freshly dug grave in the backyard of my neighbor's house, that I had started to think is my rapist, and may have more in store for me than even I was ready to see.

I saw him drive away in the wee hours last night and he hasn't returned. I know I can't just sit and wait for him to kill me. I must do something.

Running back into my house, I grab a knife from the kitchen block and wait for Gavin to return while huddled in a small cubby of his garage. I have to put him in this hole before I end up in it. And if this can happen before Steven gets home, then even better.

I only need to wait a few minutes, thirty, tops, before I hear the garage door rolling up. I'm still, my breath a little shaky. If there had been any doubt before about Gavin being my attacker, the freshly-dug grave in his yard settled it.

I know it was him.

Stilling my heart with deep breaths, I startle when he rushes past my hiding spot and jerks open the door leading to his back yard. He fumbles back through, and just when I'm psyched enough to make the move for attack, I realize his hands are full... with Steven.

Mother fucker.

I know what he's doing.

While he's in the yard, I make my escape. And my plan.

***

Gavin...

Waking up covered in dried mud and crusty blood is not on my top ten. And I know better than to do that. I should have come in and headed straight for the shower.

Exhaustion is no joke.

I think instantly about Hannah being concerned for Steven now. I wonder how she's handling it. I waste no time getting in the shower now, in case part of her worry brings her here. At least I had the wherewithal to toss the bag in the fire last night.

The water finally runs clear and my head is a little less scrambled. No regrets, but definitely some things were learned that only in hindsight became realized. I don't want to dwell on that, though. My OCD would not handle it well if I got into thinking of all the things that could have gone differently, and what the outcome would be if there was a change in what had happened. Best to keep on with the task in front of me.

Hannah.

I'm not good for her, and I'm not stupid enough to think I am. She sure as fuck isn't good for me, and I have no idea what I want from her, only that I definitely *do* want from her.

I hope she is the type to run into the arms of the closest man instead of the opposite, all would be for not if I turned her into a celibate nun.

She has a reserved appearance, but the look in her eyes and the way she moves her body is something else entirely. As if she's never had what she truly needed and is just begging for it, while not really knowing she is. She's a fucking conundrum. And it fucks up my head.

***

Hannah doesn't make an appearance at my house for two days. It relieves me to know she doesn't send anyone over here to ask questions about Steven's disappearance, but it irks me that she doesn't want to utilize my shoulder for her tears.

Her eyes are dry, but red rimmed and puffy when I open the door for her. Without an actual invite, she walks inside and plops down on the big overstuffed couch.

She starts without a preamble, "Weird question, but you wouldn't happen to know where Steven is?"

"What? What do you mean?" I'll be playing the role of dumbest man ever alive.

"You don't watch the news, I guess," she tucks her feet under her ass without removing her shoes, and I'm hardly able to keep the annoyance from my face. Luckily, she doesn't seem to notice as she continues without pause. "His car was found burned. I haven't seen him since Wednesday morning... Tuesday night really, I was asleep when he'd left." She shakes her head at her rambling so she can refocus her thoughts. "I think something might have happened to him. But the police aren't taking it seriously, even after I told them that I had been raped, inside my own house, only a few weeks prior to that. Fucking assholes." Her cheeks flush with what I can imagine is anger.

I forget my act briefly. "Uh, no, I guess I'm not really a news watcher. What do you think it means?" I suppose I salvaged it.

I sit in the chair next to her, instead of opting for the couch with her, thinking it better to keep what distance I can for now, especially while her fingers are tapping agitatedly.

My hand takes a lesson in the absolutely-don't-fucking-do-that book and lands right on her knee. So exasperating, since I thought I was clear with myself about keeping the boundaries.

My eyes worriedly search hers, knowing this could be the thing that ruins it all, but I am fucking compelled to keep it resting there in case she thinks it's acceptable.

Her face softens and she puts her hand over top mine. I'm shocked more than anything, my nerves cause my palm to sweat under hers as we sit here, both curious why the fuck this is happening.

She stands and rushes to the door suddenly, stopping with her fingers on the handle. "You'll let me know if you hear anything from him, won't you?"

"Absolutely," I stay on the chair, exactly as she left me, unable to make a move, trying not to scare her off. She knows as well as I do, something just happened, and I'm going to let her come to me. That is, if she's quick about it.

**

Hannah...

That fucking fucker! If I hadn't known what I do about him, I might have believed him and asked for help looking for my dead husband he's got buried in his fucking backyard. Piece of shit liar.

I had called the police, did my best to convey my hurt and worry over my missing husband without saying what I know about the whole thing. I had to do it that way. I can't have the police thinking that Gavin and I were in this together. Who knows what he has in his house to incriminate me? He could have been planning this for a long time. We've been neighbors for three years and I've only recently learned he's a vile, revolting, outrageous, fuck bag.

I couldn't come right out and tell the police about Gavin. I have to keep what I know about the grave in his yard secret until I know what to do with it. I got everything I needed when I looked at him today, I know it's me he wants out of all of this.

He was apprehensive and nervousness—his eyes pleading like a dog who piddled on the floor. Instinctively begging for forgiveness, while hoping you don't flick his nose.

It is exactly the admission I had needed to proceed. He deserves no pity or forgiveness. Gavin is not an overly excited dog with a loose bladder. He is just a pathetic man, capable of rape and murder to satisfy what he desires, without the integrity to remain human.

I've never given him anything to suggest I might be interested in him. Never let on that his being interested in me would be reciprocated. I wonder if that's why he didn't approach me like a normal person, he didn't even flirt with me. Just went right to rape and then murder. All while thinking he's playing it cool next door.

And now, I have to pretend I don't know any of this, and let him have what he wants. Then, I can take what I need.

Vengeance.

Nine

Hannah...

I need to get free of Gavin, and to do that I must bring him closer to me. It's got to seem natural to him. I don't want to show my cards before I'm ready.

I know now it's me he watches from his window. Before, I could think it were a hundred other things that had his attention. Not anymore.

I've decided it best for my plan to spend more time in the backyard sun bathing and managing all the spring flowers. It lets me keep eyes on him too, while playing into his obsession. Escalating things to point they are now has taken patience. I'm topless, which I only started doing recently, showing him I'm a new woman since Steven 'left', a sexually enlightened woman.

I give him about five minutes of that, it's all I can stand, before I head back inside.

The doorbell is chiming as I close the sliding door.

Jogging to the front of the house, I'm confused to see Gavin, since I could make him out in his window behind my sunglasses enjoying himself quite surely.

"Oh, hey, come on in." With a cheery smile, I wonder how, to him, seems real, I usher him inside. Sitting next to him on the couch, my skin crawls, and the vile reminder of what he's done to me is left unspoken on the tip of my tongue. If I weren't so sun-warmed I'd have goosebumps from revulsion.

"Just checking in. No news yet?" his eyes flicker to my chest, clad only in my bikini top.

"Nothing," shaking my head like the grieving wife I'm supposed to be and not the vengeful bitch he's made me. Pretending not to notice his balled fist, fighting some disgusting urge he's having.

It should worry me, but the few occasions we've spent time together after Steven's murder have been free of any threatening behavior. Leading me to believe I'm ok for now. Not that I don't have more locks on my doors and windows, a top-notch security system, and a shit-ton of weapons planted around the house for protection. Because I do.

"You don't think he had someone on the side, do you? I mean, he was gone frequently enough to find someone else. Maybe he just left me." Wringing my hands like any woman worried she's not good enough to keep her man, I watch his expression as he tries to see if this alleged infidelity from Steven could work to his advantage.

"You know, Hannah, *I* honestly couldn't imagine treating you that way, if you were mine. But I wouldn't put it past Steven."

I hold my eyes in place, instead of letting them roll like they so desperately need to. Not only has he implied that I'd been cheated on and abandoned, he's said that he would never do me like that. Prince fucking Charming.

Shyly, I say, "really," looking doe-eyed and hopeful for reassurance—the typical strategy to get a boy to think you're susceptible to his tactics.

His hand takes mine and I relax so he can. "It would be impossible to find something better than you."

"So maybe Steven didn't run off with someone?" Feigning hopefulness, I watch his annoyance tick inside his face. Weird how that same sentiment would not be true for my husband who *obviously* ran away from me. Another eye roll averted.

"Like, I said, I can only speak for myself, and what I would and wouldn't do if you were mine. I can't speak for him, but he's not here, so maybe that is speaking for him."

"It does feel more like he ran off. I think I could sense it if something bad had happened to him. Plus, he is too smart for that," *i.e. you are so smart getting one over on him*. "He was distancing himself for a while," *i.e. I'm so fucking lonely*. "I am not the same girl since that man broke in my house and raped me." *i.e. maybe that's good for you*.

"Come here," pulling me into his arms and pressing my head to his chest. I fight my whole body's need for escape, rationalizing that this would be as good a time as any for me to just kill him. But then I remember what I'm actually doing and surrender to his hold. I don't hug back, that wouldn't be natural right now, but I do nestle my face into his chest. Giving just enough for him to latch on to, and closing the gap between us.

I pull away, keeping my eyes down shyly, reluctance implied.

He lifts my chin to make our eyes meet, fingers lingering near my throat. I can see the eagerness in his enlarged pupils. Fear turns my blood cold, my near nakedness becoming hazardous. I think right then that he might rape me again if I let this go on. Maybe he'd put me in the hole with Steven.

Panic stricken; I realize now that this charade needs to move faster to remain on my terms. He doesn't care about me getting over Steven in a timely manner. His delusions have him thinking something that is illogical and irrational, never to be understood by me. He just wants what he wants.

Carefully, and with a bravery I'm uncertain will last, I pull him by his hand to my front door. "If I don't get rid of you right now, I might get myself in trouble." A smile that tells him he knows what I mean and a flirty shove gets him outside. Thankfully, he stays there.

I can see a little flicker of bad-guy, but he walks a few feet before turning to me again, "I could keep a secret."

I almost slam the door.

Ten

I have Gavin over every night for a week, slowly building a believable attraction to him, dinners, movies. Tonight, a perfectly timed kiss that I tell him bashfully shouldn't have happened, followed by a hasty goodbye.

Tomorrow is the time. He'll buy whatever I throw his way, he's demented, and desperate enough to fall for it.

***

Getting out of the bed this morning is grueling, the sun comes quicker than I want it to; I haven't slept in days. Anticipation has me more anxious than usual. The stress of a murdering rapist right next door with his sights set on yours truly, is wearing on me. The loss of my husband hasn't even been thoroughly grasped. I've had no time to decompress and deal with my life. Just this plan and all it encompasses. It's become my life and I'm hoping I can get back to my old one very soon.

I spend just shy of an hour in the shower, after giving Gavin some provocative exhibition time in the garden to watch me from his pervert tower. I'm hoping it gave him just enough foreplay to rile him up so he's off his game, and not sharp enough to pick up any contradictions I may fumble today. I'm hoping all this effort will send him the right signals, and that I won't have to spell it all out for him.

I text his phone, and when he comes to the door in response to it, I think I may have gone overboard with the nudist show from earlier.

The hungry, eager look on his face makes me throw out the plan of taking it slowly and enticing him into my bedroom seductively. Instead, I grab hold of him and pull his body to mine, kissing him with all the promise of a good time. It feels like he wants to devour and ravage me. He's ready.

Walking us toward my bedroom, removing each other's clothes along the way. He lands heavy on my mattress after a little shove from me. Seeing him naked and hard on my bed forces a roll of nausea that I have to choke down. Climbing his body slowly until I have him under me, grinding his lap, his hardness pressing against my pussy.

Gavin looks ready to explode in a mix of emotions and load of hot come. He reaches for me, tries to touch my bare chest, but I grab his wrists and force them over his head. Excitement at my confidence flares in his eyes and I know I won't have anything to worry about when I reach for the restraints to wrap his wrists. He's definitely receptive to this.

He doesn't react at all until the click locks his arm to the bedpost. I settle his surprise with distraction by sliding along his cock, pulling his other arm into position and latching him in while moving up and down his shaft.

Keeping him off my true objective, I enclose my mouth around his cock and it eagerly twitches inside, swelling thicker, I taste the subtle hint of his salty eagerness as it hits my tongue.

Sucking and slurping like I belong in porn, my theatrics making the actresses in them seem amateur. I watch his face as I take two fingers and swirl them around my tongue then, slowly drawing his dick back into my mouth, I push those fingers up his ass. His eyes go wide, but I suck harder, giving him no time to oppose. Fucking inside his ass gradually to help him get acquainted with it. I feel him responding to it all.

I hook my fingers and fuck him, his dick deep in my throat. He moans, writhing into both areas of pleasure. Fucking his ass harder and harder while my mouth can taste him get right on the edge. Gavin gasping for breath, holding on to what dignity he can while reveling in the magic feeling I'm able to give him.

There's an instant where, if you're observant enough, you can feel the subtlest shift in a man's body, his surrender to the release.

Instead of giving Gavin his, I abruptly break all contact with him. "Hannah, please, one more second. I'm not done." The frantic desperation is apparent in his whining voice, sounding like I've just ruined his life. He's begging me to let him have his climax. Instead, I watch as his come dribbles out of his dick anticlimactically.

"Woah, Hannah, that was mean," he laughs nervously, and maybe a little embarrassed, by what just happened.

"Was it meaner than anything you've done?" I keep my tone light. My words don't seem to register to him, not while he's got all that tension in his balls.

Climbing off the bed, I say, "You just sit back and relax. I have something far better in mind." He watches me in a haze of equal parts confusion and hopefulness. I get the box I compiled just for this occasion, pulling out a soft scarf, I climb up him again. Giving him my nipple to suck, I moan for him while wrapping it tightly across his face.

"Don't worry, Gavin, I'm going to let you finish, I just want to play first."

Muffled words I don't listen to happen behind his face covering. They stop abruptly when he feels my fingers, cool with lube, reach between his legs again.

"Don't be nervous, you're going to love this."

His words begin to slur as he continues to try speaking, I can't make out a single syllable. His body begins to lose the ability to hold him in position and his legs drop. When his head lulls to the side finally, I know he's out.

I dress quickly. Loading him onto the blanket on the floor so I can drag him into position. Tugging him through my house is easy, the wooden floors are smooth. When I get him out the backdoor the grass makes it a bit harder to maneuver him. Luckily our side gates share a connecting wall so I don't need to make a scene. Just a bit more and I have him where I want him.

Ass up, face down, and ready to receive my full treatment. I shove hard, and the large object enters him. I fuck him with it aggressively, tearing his insides, the lube mingling with the blood from his fissured hole.

He's deeply unconscious, which I regret, but I can't have any marks of a struggle. I have to make this look real and hopefully self-inflicted. A few more minutes of ass torture and I move on to the next level. Taking the larger object, I insert it, taking my time to position it to remain inside. It's long and the circumference is a bit hard to work with, but I manage to get it inserted, lodging it deep inside so none remains to be seen then I pull out his legs, leaving him in a prone position.

I head inside his house, with the keys from his pocket and a pair of gloves from mine and set the scene.

Eleven

"Sir, hold still. Stop fighting."

I don't know what happened at Hannah's house, I'm about to have the best nut of my life— who would have thought a couple fingers in the ass would have made it so much more intense?—and the next thing I know I'm waking up hand cuffed to a hospital bed. The middle of that is gone.

Did she fuck me into a heart-attack?

A stroke?

That doesn't explain the cuffs.

"What the fuck is going on here? Someone better start explaining shit to me. Where's Hannah?" I can probably get some answers from her.

A cop comes through the door abruptly telling me to keep it down.

I try to sit up, the shackles make it impossible to move even an inch. "I just want to know what the fuck is going on. Why are there cuffs?"

No answer from the cop because the two nurses that burst in tell me to calm down again. It seems the only words I'm going to get.

As calmly as possible, I ask again, "What is going on here?"

"You needed medical attention," the doctor says.

"Ok, what happened? Why the cuffs?" again, nice and slowly so I get a fucking answer.

"You're under arrest." The cop blurts out.

"Why?"

"Your neighbor," the cop starts, but I cut him off.

"That was consensual. She asked me over." That bitch, well, I know this isn't going to stick. This whole thing feels excessive nonetheless.

"Dead people can't give consent."

"What the fuck?! I didn't do anything to her, if she's dead, that's on her." I'm frantically trying to both, understand the situation, and defend myself.

"Listen, you sick fuck, you just wait until the sergeant gets here, he'll get you all up to speed, read you your rights and whatnot."

I instantly hate this guy; he keeps looking at me like he's disgusted.

"Officer, can I have you step aside, I need to evaluate him." The doctor steps in front of me and lifts the sheet once the officer is out of the way.

"What the fuck? What are you doing?" I don't even know where I'm injured but it doesn't feel right for him to be exposing my dick to the room.

"I'm just checking to make sure you're not hemorrhaging again."

"What happened?" I'm terrified. What the fuck… hemorrhaged? I wait for him to finish, since it doesn't seem like I'll get an answer while he's down there.

"Everything looks good, you just need to stay put, no moving around, the donut is here to keep you off your butt."

Confusion and embarrassment swirl inside my head. "Why do I have to stay off my butt?"

The question was for the doctor, but the cop answers. "You don't get to play stupid, you sick fucker. You just sit there and wait."

"I want to know what's wrong with me! How does this have anything to do with why I'm in handcuffs?" I just want a straight answer, and I don't care who it comes from, so I direct the question to the whole room.

Snidely, the cop says, "Well sir, I will say there are detectives in your backyard right now, uncovering the rest of him."

Him?

Steven.

I'm able to hide my shock, but the bewilderment in his choice of words has me compelled to ask, "What do you mean...the rest?"

"You think you can just come into the hospital with an arm from a dead man shoved up your ass so far you need surgery to get it out, and we wouldn't go looking for the rest of him?"

"The arm...?" I stutter.

"You're actually lucky your neighbor heard you shouting from your backyard, you could have died."

"My neighbor?"

Hannah.

"She came when you were shouting, saw the bloody mess you were in. Said she thought the guy who raped her had made his way to your house. Called the cops. I was first on the scene. I got there and took you right over here to the hospital. I waited to see if you'd pull through. Then the doc here informed me that you were fucking body parts. And here we are."

**

𝓗𝒶𝓃𝓃𝒶𝒽...

I couldn't have gotten away with Gavin's murder. Steven had just gone missing, assumed foul play. It would have looked like I had a hand in both. I had to come up with something else. So, the night Gavin had buried Steven, I dug a piece of him up and froze it.

I may be sick, but if you take everything away from someone, they've got nothing to lose.

The trial was quick, he took the stand in his defense and swore it was me who did all of it. The jury didn't buy it for a second, it only seemed to

122

make him more repugnant. I guess getting caught with an arm up your butt doesn't win you any friends. Maybe it will in prison though, he's got at least twenty-five years to find some.

The end.

Thank you for reading

More by Rayne:

The Other Place

Boys Will Be Boys

Collecting Rayne

(a collection of the first 8 stories, including)

My Christmas Story

Degenerate

The Boy

Devour

Retaliation

XXX

app

The Embalmer

Printed in Great Britain
by Amazon